JESSICA'S BOX

For my family

PC

First published in the UK in 2020
by New Frontier Publishing Europe Ltd
Uncommon, 126 New King's Road, London, SW6 4LZ
www.newfrontierpublishing.co.uk
ISBN: 978-1-912858-47-7

Designed by Celeste Hulme

Printed and bound in China
1 3 5 7 9 10 8 6 4 2

JESSICA'S BOX

Peter Carnavas

NEW FRONTIER PUBLISHING

Jessica's mind was too busy
for sleep.

Her thoughts were already with
tomorrow.

And when tomorrow came,
everybody was excited.

'I remember my first day...'
started Grandpa.

'You'll have a great time,'
said Dad.

'You're going to make plenty
of friends,' said Mum.

Plenty of friends, thought Jessica.
She was going to make sure of that.

At first, nobody noticed.

Plenty of friends, thought Jessica.
She was going to make sure of that.

At first, nobody noticed.

But by lunchtime, a crowd of curious children had gathered.
Jessica reached into the box.

'Ta-DAAA!'

Some children laughed.

Some tried not to.

Others just walked away.

'What's so good about a
stuffed bear?'
a small boy asked.

'Lots of things,' said
Jessica.

'Lots of ...things.'

Jessica told Mum all about her horrible lunchtime
and how she didn't make any friends.

'You'll just have to try something else,' said Mum.

So after thinking it over with Doris,
Jessica did try something else.

CUPCAKES!

What a marvellous idea.
The hungry hands scooped them up and,
just as quickly, disappeared.

Not even a *thank you*?

Jessica and Doris
thought even harder
this time.

And as Doris cleaned up the crumbs from the box,
a clever idea crept into Jessica's head.

'What's her name?'

'She's beautiful!'

'Can I have a pat?'

Everybody wanted to talk to Jessica.
It felt wonderful.

But it didn't last.
Within minutes the school
groundskeeper arrived.

'Can't bring dogs to school,'
he said, as he snatched Doris
and drove her home.

It was Dad's turn to talk to
Jessica that night.

The following day, Jessica didn't take
anything in her box.

She just wanted
to disappear.

'Found you!'

Jessica peered out of the box.
'Now you have to find me,' said the boy.
'Count to ten.'

Jessica wondered for a moment.
Had she made a friend?
There was only one thing to do.

At home, the family was delighted to hear about Jessica's new friend.

Grandpa leaned in close and said, 'You must have had something very special in your box today.'

Jessica smiled and said, 'I did.'